TITLE

JERK AT FIRST SIGHT

Chapter One

Laura was at that point used to burning through the entirety of her evenings alone, so this one shouldn't be any unique, if not for her birthday. She had quite recently returned home from an unpleasant day at work, where nobody is familiar with this significant date, in light of the fact that Laura never told them. Furthermore she had an awesome motivation to conceal it from them.

It was on her fifth birthday celebration that Laura's dad suddenly left the nation and deserted his family. Right away, they revealed him as absent, yet they before long had found proof that validated his goals: he had taken all their cash from their family records and left them with an immense obligation. Obviously, he had been heaping it for quite a long time, without their insight, because of a betting habit that they didn't realize he had.

A couple of years after the fact, somebody perceived Laura's father via web-based media. He was living in an outlandish country, with another spouse and children. They announced the case to the police, looking for equity, at the same time, until this day, her dad has never been found. Due to such conditions, Laura's mom, Linda, needed to maintain three sources of income at the same time to pay the immense obligation.

Since Linda was continually working constantly, Laura was left with her grandma more often than not. Accordingly, all her birthday recollections were with her. Laura's grandma would make her a little birthday cake and, solely after her mom showed up from work, would they all sing her a cheerful birthday. Tragically, her grandma spent away two years prior, transforming those minutes into self-contradicting recollections.

Laura tossed her keys on top of the doorway table and undressed her jacket, draping it on the divider. It was cold outside and since she doesn't claim a vehicle or even have a driver's permit, Laura needs to take the transport and the tram home, consistently. Rapidly, she removed her incredibly awkward shoes and tenderly kneaded her feet, permitting them to move. Her feet were harming like hellfire today.

She headed higher up and quickly went into the washroom. She removed her garments and started filling the bath with warm water. Laura was frantically wanting for a long shower right now. She was wanting to quietness the musings that generally torment her on this day, February thirteenth. Nonetheless, she realized that her unwinding second would ultimately get demolished in the following not many hours. Regardless of whether all she needed to do was lay inside that hot bath, Laura knew that her mom generally visits her on her birthday.

It was a custom that the two of them had, and presumably the one to focus on. Normally, Linda prepares them supper and afterward goes through the whole evening with Laura until she should return home. Some of the time, they scarcely even talk, however basically they are together. Laura realizes that Linda's nonattendance is exclusively her dad's shortcoming, however she can't resist the urge to feel separated from her mom. The two will in any case talk routinely, however not with the closeness that Laura would like.

Laura doesn't have any companions, not even working. She converses with certain individuals sometimes, however that is it. She doesn't recall the last time she went through a night out with somebody other than her mom. What's more indeed, she realizes that a portion of that is her own problem for not putting forth a greater amount of an attempt to associate with individuals, however she additionally faults the shortfall of her folks for that. Without her father present, and with her mom missing constantly, Laura immediately became acclimated to being separated from everyone else. Back in school, she wouldn't coexist with different children. Truth be told, she loathed them, since they all had cheerful families back home and she didn't.

The mirror in the washroom started to get hazy and transformed the reasonable picture of Laura's body into a basic lady's outline. Perhaps her body wasn't that unique in relation to the normal ladies' body all things considered. With the state of her body gradually vanishing from the washroom reflect, Laura imagined what her ideal figure would resemble. What started resembling a superior adaptation of herself on that hazy mirror, immediately transformed into a hot man's body.

Laura turned away from the mirror, wanting to jerk off immediately.

"However, for what reason am I so desolate?", she.

The way that she never at any point had lost her virginity and that she was at that point turning 32, was beginning to burden her. At long last, she got into the bath and switched off the running water. The water was all in all too warm, yet she couldn't have cared less. She simply needed a couple of moments of unwinding before her mom showed up. She tossed a shower bomb into the bath, which promptly transformed the water into a beautiful and pleasant smelling sea.

With the ambiguous outline of the hot man's body still at the forefront of her thoughts, Laura made her hand slide through her neck, her bosoms, and her midsection, until her fingertips contacted her labia. Unexpectedly, the doorbell ran, halting her.

"Not at the present time!", she groaned delicately.

Linda had the keys to her place, so Laura figured she could wait and partake in her decent shower while her mom got in. Be that as it may, she was off-base. Her telephone began ringing and Laura got it. Fortunately, it was waterproof, so she could simply settle on the decision inside the bath with her wet fingers. On the cell phone's screen, "Mother" was written in all covers. She addressed the call with an extremely disturbed tone:

"What?", she inquired.

"Where are you?", Linda asked Laura. "No doubt about it.", she said.

"Indeed, I am.", Laura answered. "I'm simply cleaning up.".

"Sorry! Yet, I failed to remember my keys.", Linda reported delicately.

Laura feigned exacerbation and hanged up the telephone without saying another word. The way that she currently needed to escape the shower and go open the entryway, was not satisfying her by any stretch of the imagination. With an excessive lot of exertion, Laura at long last escaped the warm bath and ventured out into the cool washroom floor. For set on her shoes and snatched a towel, folding it over her wet body.

She could feel her legs shuddering from the cold, so she went ground floor quick. Her home was little yet sufficiently comfortable for simply her. On the least floor, the front entryway leads into a little entrance. On the left, it's the kitchen, and, on the right, there's the flight of stairs that drives higher up. Forward, it's the family room, a little but agreeable spot to be. Right close to the front room, there is a washroom and, higher up, there are two rooms and another restroom.

Chapter Two

Laura opened the front entryway and saw that her mom was addressing a manly figure. It was at that point dull outside, so she was unable to see who the individual was, yet she realized that his voice sounded natural. At the point when Linda understood that she was at the entryway pausing, she inquired as to whether he might want to come inside, to which he immediately answered no.

The peculiar figure moved forward, drawing nearer to the entryway and uncovering his character to Laura. With his face presently illuminated by the family room lights, she could at last remember him. Turns out that it was James, her chief. James Harris was the current CEO of Gold Owl, the organization that she worked for. Notwithstanding the odd name, Gold Owl was a lofty and lavish organization that had practical experience in mining gold and afterward offering it to sumptuous adornments brands across the world. They were awesome at how they treated, additionally one of the most rewarding organizations in the entire country.

James' dad established the organization himself and ran it for a really long time until he at last resigned a year prior. The organization was notorious all of the time for paying their staff the lowest pay permitted by law, while everybody in higher positions was benefitting a ridiculous measure of cash. It was likewise an exceptionally harmful climate to work at, or perhaps Laura can't coexist with anybody there.

"Glad birthday, Laura!", wished James, halting right external her entryway.

"Much thanks to you.", Laura answered.

That was whenever that she first saw James outside of work, and there was something other than what's expected with regards to him now. He wasn't wearing his extravagant costly suits. All things considered, he was donning a cushy dark sweater and some close dark pants. Laura could even swear that he looked more youthful.

She never given an excess of consideration to James previously, and, without a doubt, she never seen him like she's looking at this point. He appeared to be 100% of the time to be so arrogant and was scarcely even present at the organization. However, this time, Laura was liking his magnificence: his sweater and tight jeans were flaunting his solid form; his light earthy colored complexion was sparkling delicately; his earthy colored short hair with lighter features, was permitting his lovely face to be seen; and his stunning blue eyes were sparkling.

"Laura! Mr James was here seeing a few properties around here and he inquired as to whether I really wanted any assistance getting inside.", informed Linda. "He was so kind!", she proceeded.

"She just failed to remember her keys.", explained Laura with an off-kilter grin toward the end.

"Indeed. She told me." James uncovered. "Were you showering?", he asked, pointing at her body, covered with a towel.

Humiliated, she let out an off-kilter snicker and attempted to cover her body more, extending the towel.

"Indeed.", Laura affirmed.

James giggled gracelessly as well.

"Indeed, I ought to get rolling now.", he said. "It was great seeing you, Laura.".

James pivoted and bid farewell to Linda: "It was great gathering you too Ms. Jones!". On the off chance that Laura wasn't feeling desolate sufficient only a couple of moments prior, she most certainly was presently. Yet, James could never be a counterpart for her. She believes that James is way out of her association and that dating her own manager would be something beyond reach.

At long last, Linda ventured inside, shutting the entryway behind her. There was no hello among them, not so much as a kiss or an embrace. They didn't have that sort of closeness, along these lines, a straightforward welcome is sufficient.

"I will complete washing… " reported Laura, previously climbing the steps.

"Alright." Agreed her mom, while she made a beeline for the kitchen.

When Laura got once more into the restroom, she quickly inundated herself in the serious trouble once more. Presently, she could at last unwind. At last agreeable, Laura shut her eyes. In any case, rather than seeing just haziness, she had the picture of James in her mind. She got surprised and woken her up to attempt to shake that picture out of her mind.

She could as of now feel the desire of her body, asking to contemplate him and give it some delight, however she wouldn't yield. Essentially not right now, since her mom was in the house. Likewise, Laura was not ready to fantasize about her rich chief. Disappointed, she escaped the warm bath and went into her room, which was perfect before the restroom. She changed into her most agreeable night robe, all things considered, it was still her birthday. What's more, despite the fact that she never needs to commend it, she actually blames it so as to do anything she desires.

As she was going first floor, she could as of now smell the food being prepared. Her mom was in the kitchen, making her cherished dish for supper, as she generally does when it's Laura's birthday. It was only a few basic hand crafted tacos, however her mom was a remarkable expert at making the best tacos on the planet. Basically that is the means by which Laura sees it.

The TV in the kitchen was turned on, and her mom was watching a syndicated program, something not Laura's style. She would prefer to observe a portion of her dream and loathsomeness TV shows. But, since she appreciated her mom's organization, she would watch it this time. She sat in one of the seats of her eating table, watching her mom cook.

"How are you, Laura?", her mom inquired.

"I'm accomplishing something useful.", she answered. "However, work is being a piece upsetting."

"Please accept my apologies to hear that... I thought your manager appeared to be great.", Linda said.

"I couldn't say whether he's great or not.", Laura said.

"What difference would it make?"

"Since I scarcely even get to see him. He's never at the organization, he simply recruits others to do his occupation for him."

"That is a disgrace."

Linda switched off the oven and Laura snatched the dishes to prepare the table. The food smelled so decent that unexpectedly Laura could eat more than she ordinarily would have the option to. Or on the other hand, maybe, that was because of the way that James was as yet at the forefront of her thoughts and that she needed it to disappear. The syndicated program finished and the news broadcast began. The two of them took a seat at the table, confronting the TV while eating. Before the end, they had completed the process of eating without saying a solitary word to one another.

Laura started to put the messy dishes inside the washer, while Linda made a move to uncover something:

"There's a motivation behind why I didn't bring my keys."

"What is it?", asked Laura. She was beginning to feel that something awful had happened to her mom and she felt her heart throbbing. Indeed, even with the substantial distance among them, Laura cherished her mom like some other girl would, and was exceptionally thankful that she landed those positions to place food on the table and pay for her dad's obligation.

"The bank took the house... ", Linda unfortunately uncovered.

Laura could feel the trouble in her voice and in the event that her mom wasn't crying yet, it was simply because she was holding herself from going off the rails mentally on her little girl's birthday.

"Why?", Laura asked, concerned.

"I got a letter from the bank the year before. I wasn't paying the obligation as quick as they needed me to.".

"Same difference either way."

"Since I lost one of my positions the year before. Furthermore I'm too old to even consider securing another position... "

"Mother! You out to have been let me know this!", shouted Laura.

Linda was gazing at the ground, profoundly embarrassed about what she was at last uncovered to her girl.

"I would have rather not disturbed you... ", Linda clarified.

"For what reason would you disturb me? I would've helped you!"

"They came to the house today to remove me and I could snatch a small bunch of stuff, so I failed to remember your keys."

Laura took a full breath. She was amazingly annoyed with her mom for staying quiet about that, yet she comprehended her mom's motivations to do as such. She was likewise beginning to fault herself for not minding her mom all the more regularly. Perhaps on the off chance that she wasn't really narrow minded, she could've forestalled this entire circumstance.

"Where are you going to remain now?", asked Laura.

Linda stopped, as yet confronting the ground. She obviously didn't have a solution to that inquiry.

"You can remain here.", promptly offered Laura.

It was the least she could do, and surprisingly that wasn't to the point of compensating for her nonappearance.

"No, no. I can't!", Linda rejected.

"Indeed, you can. Also you clearly will!"

Linda at last raised her head to check out Laura. Her demeanor was of significant trouble. Laura turned on the dishwasher and switched off the TV. She took her mom's hand and hauled her higher up. The two of them climbed the steps at a sluggish speed, and Linda didn't know of what was happening, yet she went with it. At the point when the two of them showed up at the higher up passageway, Laura opened her visitor's room entryway, uncovering an extremely coordinated and insignificant room. At its middle, there was a flawlessly made bed.

"You are constantly invited here.", said Laura. "Furthermore despite the fact that we haven't been just about as close as we would like, there's nothing in this world that I would like more than you remaining here with me."

Linda's eyes were out of nowhere loaded up with affection and were currently gleaming.

"Much thanks to you.", she said delicately.

The two of them went down the stairs to get the main two sacks that Linda had the option to carry with her on the transport. They put everything down in the visitor's room and Linda before long rested. It was really late as of now, so Laura would before long follow. Above all, she needed to go ground floor and take out the dishes from the washer, putting away them back into the cupboards.

Whenever she was done, and before she went to her room, she opened the other room entryway and looked at her resting mother. She seemed quieted and loose, even in spite of all that she must've been feeling for these beyond couple of days. Then, at that point, at last, Laura rested.

Chapter Three

Without precedent for quite a while, Laura had longed for a man. What's more it wasn't with any customary person, it was with James fucking Harris.

"For what reason did it need to be him?", she asked herself.

She got up as fast as possible, in a frantic endeavor to forget about him. It was just 5.30 am, so she needed to switch off the alert that she had recently set for 6 am. Laura went to the restroom and washed up. She didn't require over five minutes in length, since she actually had James at the forefront of her thoughts and that was at that point making her insane.

Laura went into her mom's room and saw that she was all the while resting. Since she had spare time, Laura chose to head first floor a make a legitimate breakfast. Most occasions, she is continuously running so late that she simply eats a bar of cereal en route. In any case, today, she needed to give a few avocado impromptu speeches.

It was as yet dull outside, and extremely hazy as well, so Laura turned on the lights. She likewise chose to turn on the TV, however she quieted the sound so it wouldn't wake her mom. It didn't take long to give the impromptu speeches, and, whenever she was finished eating, she returned higher up to prepare for work.

Whenever she was done and prepared to take off, she chose to go mind her mom only one final time and ensured that she was all the while dozing. It was 6.30 am presently, and the transport left at 7, however she actually needed to walk the whole way to the bus station.

She took one of her extra keys and left it on top of the table, for her mom to utilize. She then, at that point, got her jacket and taken off the entryway. The mist outside was at that point clearing up, however it was still a piece difficult so that Laura might see the way. She needs to stroll about a mile until she arrives at the bus station.

Presently, Laura lives in Westerford, a peripheric city that encompasses Coldlyn, which is the enormous city. She moved to her present home when she was 25 after she had found a new line of work at a cheap food chain and figured out how to set aside up sufficient cash to pay lease for an entire year. After two years, at 27, she got her present situation at Gold Owl.

Laura was more than happy with her life. She didn't actually need anything more. She had sufficient cash to pay for her home, for her food and for her beloved books, games, and motion pictures. Her main wishes were to make more companions and who knows whether she could at any point need to have a sweetheart.

The bus station just had two additional individuals pausing, so she plunked down on the seat. One reason that Laura decided to live in Westerford, was on the grounds that it is way less swarmed than the large city, and a lot more secure as well. Here, she is only one hour from Coldlyn and she can in any case live in harmony.

Today was February fourteenth, Valentine's day. Laura loathed this date. In addition to the fact that it was only the day after her birthday, however she likewise thought this day was intended to cause her to feel substandard for not having a beau. Regardless of whether now and then she feels forlorn, she doesn't need a man in her life right now. Perhaps on the grounds that, where it counts, she is worried about the possibility that that they will wind up like her dad: misleading her and at last leaving her.

She got on the transport and saw an engagement proposition's. Obviously, Laura promptly turned her eyes over. She chose to go demonstration the back, where nobody at any point sits, so she could avoid each and every individual who was infatuated.

"This day is abhorrent.," she thought.

Her occupation was worrying her recently. There was an excess of work to be done, and they didn't have as many staff chipping away at it as they ought to. Mulling over everything, that was all James' shortcoming. He was forcing her group to finish the work in an uncaring stretch of time. It was silly! Laura comprehended the reason why nobody at the organization was ready to revolt against them and request a greater check. Everybody feared them. One letter from the board and she would undoubtedly never work again in a similar field. That is the force of one of the country's greatest organizations.

She likewise didn't have any desire to lose her employment, regardless of whether she at times felt that it was a lot for her. She really wanted the cash and she previously had a daily practice set up. Changing all that presently would noble motivation superfluous uneasiness. Following a 30 minutes transport drive, Laura showed up at her stop. Presently, all she needed to do was walk a large portion of a mile to the metro station. A many individuals would rather avoid public transportations, however Laura was driving this way for her entire life, so it previously felt normal to her. She even became acclimated to the frightening individuals and presently she effectively overlooks them. The metro requires 15 minutes to show up at her Coldlyn station. Then, at that point, she needs to walk an additional five minutes into the tall Gold Owl place of business.

The roads at Coldlyn were more packed today than expected. In any case, today was likewise not an ordinary Friday at any rate. There were even individuals selling blossoms and roses at each corner, and a many individuals were getting them. Laura couldn't comprehend the idea of the blossoms. She would much prefer like to be offered some wine or even a pleasant book. Blossoms can be pretty, yet they rapidly cease to exist.

Laura showed up at the workplace only a couple of moments prior, as she generally does. She would rather not give them additional hours, since they won't pay for them, yet additionally in light of the fact that she would rather not give them that advantage.

At everybody's work area this year, there was a solitary and wonderful red rose. It was a surprising thing at the workplace, so Laura pondered where the blossoms came from.

"Good day!", welcomed Emma.

Emma was an example of the rare type of person that conversed with her here, however Laura actually wouldn't call her a companion. Perhaps she could attempt to draw nearer to her, however she didn't have the foggiest idea how to do that since she has never made any companions.

"Good day.", answered Laura. "What's happening with the rose?"

"Goodness, it was James who got one for every one of the young ladies at the organization. Individuals were saying that this is whenever that he first doesn't have a date to take to his family supper."

"Along these lines, he needs to take somebody from the workplace?", Laura asked, appalled with that thought.

"He doesn't actually think often about the organization so I am not amazed.", Emma remarked.

That was presumably the most broad discussion that Laura at any point had with somebody inside the workplace, and it felt pleasant. Perhaps Emma was a decent individual, and, who knows, perhaps Laura could attempt to turn into her companion.

In any case, as of now, Laura was pondering James. She knew that consistently his family has a practice to have one of the main meals around. Fun truth, Gold Owl was supported at Valentine's day, so his family requires this day way more genuinely than every other person. The popular supper was jam-stuffed 100% of the time with superstars, significant financial specialists and it typically gets huge loads of media inclusion.

It was additionally extremely famous that James, as the awful kid he truly was, would take an alternate young lady with him consistently. Where he meets them is indistinct, yet with his appeal, it's likely wasn't that hard for him to track down a date. Laura asks why he couldn't get one this year.

In any case, attempting to entice the ladies at the workplace, as Laura would like to think, was a dirty move. She was not satisfied with this by any means. Or then again, perhaps, her sentiments were, indeed, just desire. Laura in a real sense shook her head, in a bombed endeavor to dispose of such idea. For what reason would she even be desirous of him? They don't have a clue about one another that much.

Startlingly, James passes directly before her and heads straightforwardly to his office. Her heart was mysteriously dashing at this point. He secured the entryway his office and shut every one of the blinds. Everybody was gazing. It was extremely strange to see him at his office, particularly on a day as significant as today. Something was continuing.

"Imagine a scenario where all of us are getting terminated?", said Emma, concerned.

"I don't imagine that is what's happening... ", guaranteed Laura.

Be that as it may, she wasn't altogether certain. It could occur, yet it was improbable. As Laura would see it, he was going through private matters.

James opened the entryway and called out to out Laura. She checked out him and he made a hand motion implying that she ought to get inside. Her heart was thumping such a lot of that she was unable to try and feel it any longer. She kicked up and off strolling. It was looking more like a stroll of disgrace. Everybody was watching her and she could scarcely move. She was feeling her body shuddering, however she was unable to comprehend the reason why she was so apprehensive.

She got inside his office and he advised her to close the entryway, thus she made it happen. He was sitting at his work area and made another motion communicating her to sit in the seat before him. She continued to oblige. For what reason did he bring her over? He ordinarily did nothing like that.

"How are you, Laura?", he inquired.

"I'm fine.", answered Laura. She was astounded that he even recalled her name.

"I want to ask you some help.", he said.

"Obviously.".

"I would like in the event that you kept our the previous evening experience to yourself.".

Laura found his solicitation very odd, yet it was nothing of her should be worrying about to barge in.

"Sure. I won't tell anybody.", she guaranteed him.

His eyes locked on Laura's and she could see that he wasn't just persuaded.

"It's truly not my concern... ", she added, following it with a constrained giggle, in a bombed endeavor to break the strain in the room.

"Much thanks to you for comprehension. It's simply that... I'm going through certain issues and they can't discover that I was around there.", he clarified.

"As I said, it's truly not my concern.", she continued saying, indicating that she didn't need any more data. Be that as it may, subtly, she was interested. What was he stowing away?

"Much thanks to you.", he said.

During the whole discussion, James was continuously looking squarely at Laura. Then again, she was so apprehensive with his quality that she continued to attempt to turn away.

"You can return to work presently, that is all.", he said grinning.

Laura gestured and got up. Then, at that point, James halted directly before her.

"Assuming somebody asks, simply say that I needed to ask you out to supper this evening.", he said.

She was much more apprehensive at this point. How might she let individuals know that James requested that she be his date on the main occasion of the organization? Also for what reason would he ask her, all things considered? As she would like to think, that would put individuals discussing both of them, and she didn't need that. What's more, for what reason would she decline such a greeting?

Her delay was self-evident and James saw that she was having questions.

"I will sit tight for your response.", he explained.

"How treat mean?", she asked him.

"That I really need you to be my date this evening.".

His eccentric grin toward the end, just before he opened the entryway for her to leave, drove her both crazy and energized simultaneously. First off, she was excited that the greeting was valid, yet she additionally realized that he just did that to guarantee that she kept quiet. Indeed, Laura was really furious that she could simply educate everybody at the present time. Yet, she wouldn't make it happen.

"How treated need?", Emma asked her, when she took a seat at her work area.

Rapidly, Laura understood that she was unequipped for breaking her guarantee, so she just educated Emma concerning the greeting. Emma was stunned by such information, yet so was Laura. Both of them continued discussing it for a really long time and, in no time, it was at that point noon.

"Where are you going to eat?", asked Emma.

"I simply bring my own and I eat it here while I work.", answered Laura.

Emma got up and said: "All things considered, today you are going with me to the sushi eatery."

"Gracious, no. I'm fine, truly.", Laura rejected.

"Gibberish. I'll pay!", offered Emma. "I generally go alone so I would see the value in the organization.", she said.

Laura would truly not liked to go, yet she had a miserable hearing outlook on Emma eating alone each day, so she needed to stay with her.

"OK.", Laura concurred. "However, I'm not allowing you to pay.", she added.

"We'll see regarding that... ", said Emma.

The two of them giggled and went to the café.

Chapter Four

For the first time in a long time, Laura was in a good mood. Having lunch with Emma was refreshing. They both talked the whole time, and Laura realized that Emma also didn't have any friends. Maybe they could eventually even become friends.

Once they were in the office, time flew. It was only 4 pm, but everyone was already leaving. The office was closing earlier, just like it does every year on this important date. Laura had just begun to pack her things when she was approached by James. Emma smiled at them and left.

"So… Have you considered my offer?", he asked with a quirky smile.

"I thought it was just an excuse.", Laura said.

"No. I told you that I meant it. I want you to be my date tonight."

Laura laughed. James looked at her with a serious and confused expression. He was being serious, and she couldn't understand why.

"As if.", she started. "I don't even have a dress."

"Then we'll get one.", James suggested.

His charm was undeniable. Those blue eyes were piercing her soul and his expensive black suit was flattering. James really was a dream guy, so Laura couldn't understand why he had invited her. Her silence took too long, and James took it as a yes.

"Then it's a date!", he announced. "I'll be at your house at 7.", he finished, right before leaving.

Laura was standing still and her vocal cords could not even make a sound. She picked up her bag and noticed that she was shaking. Why was she getting all nervous again? Well, this time, she could use the excuse of the dinner instead of being nervous because of him. There was no way that she would ever admit that.

Everyone would see her at the event, right by James's side. Was she ready for all that attention? Would he throw her away like a piece of garbage when the night was over? That is why she always avoided men. They have no feelings and they are always such jerks. Why didn't she refuse his request? Maybe, Laura was happy for making a new friend at work today and she let that cloud her decision. But happiness is something that she has not felt in a long time.

She got out of the building and went back to the subway station. During the ride home, both on the subway and on the bus, she kept thinking about James's true intentions with her. And what was the secret about her neighborhood that he so desperately wanted to hide?

Laura had decided that she was not going to the dinner party. When James was to arrive at her place, she would just refuse his invitation. In her mind, he would not be able to force her. But why does she feel like she, deep down, wants to go? Why does her mind keep replaying James's pretty face on a loop? Laura wanted to take the opportunity so that she could spend more time with him. But what if he rejected her?

When she arrived home, her mother was already there. It was only 5.15 pm, so she also left work earlier.

"Already home?", Laura asked her mom.

"Yes. Mr. Boone will attend the dinner later tonight. You know, your company's dinner.", she clarified.

"That's odd. He never went before, did he?", Laura asked.

Mr. Boone, or just Howard, was a businessman that grew up with Linda. He was born poor, like the rest of the people there, but then he started to run some shady businesses and mysteriously got rich. He also thinks that he is better than everyone else now, so he hired Laura's mother to be his housemaid.

"Yeah, I think so.", Linda replied.

Laura thought that it was odd, but she forgot about it. She had something else to think about. Since she was not used to having someone else home, she decided to go to her room, in order to have more privacy.

She starting thinking about saying yes to dinner. What did she have to lose? She liked the way she was feeling at lunch earlier today when she was with Emma. They were being friends. And Laura has almost forgotten what being with someone was like. If she wanted to be with James, why couldn't she go? Was she supposed to live that monotonous boring life forever? She had to take some risks at some point.

In a bold decision, she decided to get ready. First, she had to take a bath. Laura wanted to make sure that her body was smelling the best if she was going to meet all of those fancy people. And, honestly, she would also appreciate it if James liked how nice she smelled.

She went into the bathroom and picked up her best bath bomb. This one was expensive, and Laura was not sure when was she planning on using it. Well, this was the perfect chance to do so! She filled up the bathtub and placed the bath bomb in the water, which quickly dissolved and irradiated a magical scent. It was good stuff.

Laura went in and started to rub her entire body with its foam. She was going to leave home smelling wonderful. She got out of the bath and decided that she was going to curly her hair, something that she usually never does, but this was a very special occasion. By the time she was done, it was already 6.30 in the afternoon.

"Shit!", she thought.

She goes to choose her best outfit, just to realize that she had nothing that could even remotely suit such occasion. Her closet was full of oversized sweaters, leggings, workout clothes and other comfortable sweaters and pants. Not only was that what she wears to work every day, but to the grocery store too. And those two are about the only trips that she makes when she leaves the house. She doesn't go to parties, and maybe she really shouldn't attend this one either.

Suddenly, the doorbell ranged. Could it possibly be James already? Her mom opens the door and greets him, telling him to step inside. While still in her bedroom, Laura desperately dresses a green shirt and some basic dark blue jeans. There was nothing better to wear. Besides, James said that they could go buy a dress, so why wouldn't she accept that offer?

She sprayed herself with her best perfume and nearly emptied the entire bottle. Then, she put on her wedding shoes, which is just a nice pair of black shoes that she wears to every wedding she ever goes to. Finally, she got out of her bedroom and heads downstairs.

James is sitting at her kitchen table, eating something that her mother offered him.

"There you are, sweetie.", Linda says. "I baked some cookies. You didn't tell me that you were going out tonight!".

"She didn't?", James asked, surprised.

"I wasn't really sure if I wanted to go.", Laura confessed.

James got up and took a good look at Laura. Maybe she was dressing too ordinary for his liking. He, on the other hand, had a nice grey suit that irradiated to be custom made from very expensive materials. James stretched out his hand and Laura grabbed it.

"Let's go, then.", he said.

A simple goodbye to her mom was enough. Laura was happy that she was living in her house now, but it was also kind of sad that they were not spending any time together. James opened the door and signaled Laura to go first. He did the same thing in the car. It was a very expensive and beautiful car too. She is used to the smelly odor that comes from the bus seats, not to heated leather.

It was strange that they were both inside his car, driving to one of the most important parties in the state, without even knowing too much about each other. Laura knew that she felt something for him, she just could not explain it yet. But she wondered if he also felt something for her too, or was it all just an act?

"We need to go get you a dress.", James said.

"Okay.", Laura agreed.

The radio was on, but it was so low that it was barely noticeable. The dash lights were lighting his face, and Laura took a good look at him. She was incredibly attracted to him, but she felt that he would never look at her that way. She is not pretty, in her opinion.

"Why are you staring at me?", James asked, smiling.

Laura got embarrassed. She didn't even know what to say.

"I don't know...", she said.

"Is there a problem?", he asked her with a more serious tone.

"I don't know why you'd invite me.", she confessed.

"Why not?"

"Because I'm nothing like the other girls that you usually bring."

"Don't say that. You should not think so little of yourself. You are actually really pretty."

Did James just tell her that she was pretty? Okay, now her heart was ready to pop out of her chest. But what if he was just being nice and polite? He probably does not feel that way about her anyway.

"It's true. We have barely even spoken. I have a feeling that you're just using me…". Laura's tone was serious and sad. She was regretting getting in his car.

"Why would you think that?", he asked upset.

"Because you want me to keep your secret.", she revealed.

"Yes, I want you to keep my secret. But that's not why I invited you."

"Then why did you?". She sounded angry and that was making James get angry too.

"Because, for the first time in my life, I am single!", he shouted. "I can't be a failure to my family like that."

"So, you just want me to be your escort? Because being seen with a different girl every year will make your family proud?", Laura shouted.

"Yes, for my fucked-up family, that is a success!", he shouted back at her.

Laura's expression changed. She was not expecting such a response.

"Since I can remember that my father cheats on my mom with everyone!", he continued. "You don't know my father. You don't know how much he pressures me to be like him!".

"You're an adult. You control your life.", Laura said.

"I only wish that was the case."

James got sad; she could hear it in his voice. Like he was just about to burst into tears. She felt bad for him. For one second, she wanted him to cry on her lap while she massaged his head. But that was not going to happen, because she was still not okay with the fact that he was just using her.

"I don't want to go anymore.", she said.

"What? Why?"

"Are seriously still asking me that? After all of what you just said?"

"I was just being honest! That does not mean that I do not want to enjoy your company and to be with you. Otherwise, I would've just invited somebody else."

"Why would you want to be with me? I'm nobody.", she said.

"Don't say does things about yourself. You seem like a nice person and I would like to get to know you better. Can we please just go buy a dress and then you'll decide if you still want to go to the party or not."

"Okay.", she agreed.

The car was taken by silence until they finally arrived at the mall. But it was not any mall, it was one of the most expensive malls in the country. Laura has never even been there because she cannot afford to shop at any of its stores.

Chapter Five

"I can't afford this.", she said, as soon as James parked the car.

"I can", said James and got out of the car.

Laura was not that much pleased with the fact that he would be the one to gift her the dress, but she did not have much of a choice anyway. They both went into a shop that specializes in ceremony dresses and it seemed that James already knew the staff. This is probably where he brings all his dates.

They started to measure Laura's body and took her into a fitting room. It was large, filled with shiny mirrors and there was a group of people around her picking dresses and showing them to her. She liked a few, but they all had to be adjusted to her silhouette. She wasn't really feeling this whole thing. After the argument that she just had with James in the car, she was just feeling like a whore, taking advantage of him and his money. And that was not who she was.

Already fed up with her own thoughts and overwhelmed by so many dresses and people around her, she left. She picked up her clothes and ran out of the store. James saw her leaving and started to run after her but she could not stop. Laura began to feel the tears that were starting to fall down her face and she just wanted to go home, to her comfortable place.

In a matter of seconds, James grabbed her hand, stopping her.

"What happened?", he asked her.

He saw that she was crying and his expression towards her changed. He was sad for her too, so he hugged her. Laura could punch him the face because of all of what she was feeling regarding him, but she did not. She was comfortable by being held by his strong arms. She rested her face on his shoulder and placed her arms on his back. She could feel his tight muscles and she was enjoying it.

"Let's go.", he said, holding her hand and leading the way out of the mall.

Eventually, her tears had ceased. And, by the time that she was already inside the car, she felt like an idiot.

"I'm sorry...", she said.

"For what?", he asked her. "For showing me that you are an actual human being?"

"What do you mean?"

"I mean that you can feel. And I am the one who is sorry to put you in this position. I know this is too much for you... It's just that I am not used to being with someone like you. Most of the girls that date me are hollow and they only care about my status or money but not you. You're different. And that's why I like you so much.".

His eyes locked into Laura's and for just a second, she stopped breathing. He raised his hand into her face and wiped out a few tears that were still there. The touch of his hand felt magical. His piercing eyes were murdering her heart, but she was enjoying it. Maybe it was too early to say that she was falling in love, but she truly was.

"Do you still want to go to the party?", he asked her.

"Do you even have a choice?"

"I suppose that we always do."

For more that she fancied the idea of the two of them skipping the party and going somewhere else, she would feel incredibly bad about it. He already talked about how his relationship with his father was messed up, imagine how much pissed off with James he would be if he did not attend.

"No, we'll go.", she said.

"Are you sure?"

"Yeah."

But she was not. She did not even have a dress. "Screw it.", she thought. It is time to take more risks. James began driving and they arrived within a few minutes. Her heart was pounding again. The mansion was lit by big and bright spotlights and there were people coming out of their cars right on to the red carpet. She was about to be one of those people.

The flashes from the photographers were excruciating, even if they were protected by the darkened mirrors of James's car. He parked the car right in front of the entrance and instantly, everyone gathered around the car. She remembers watching this on TV. James's date was always the most interesting and talked-about moment of the night.

"This is it.", James confirmed.

Once again, Laura started shaking. Perhaps because she was wearing jeans and a shirt, or maybe it was since she was going to be featured in every magazine the day after that. James noticed that she was shivering, so he held her hand, intertwining his fingers between hers.

She looked at him, and relaxed. Somehow, she was happy that she was with him. Was that weird? Maybe. But she was feeling happy. And with a man, no less. The species that she kept avoiding for years. Perhaps, it was time to let go of all fears and just do what she feels like now. She was feeling alive, and she did not want to get rid of that feeling ever again in her life.

He opened his door and got out of the car. She waited inside while he went around to open the door for her, but she was so used to open her own door, that as an impulse, she got out of the car herself. As soon as she stepped out, her face became lit by the camera flashes and her ears were hurting from all the photographers screaming.

James stood by her and stretched out his hand, and she accepted it. They both walked the red carpet holding hands and she could not remember him doing that with any of his previous flings. Maybe this time it was different after all. She got thrilled by the idea of her being special for him, so she held his hand tighter.

They finally made inside the big hall and his mother came to greet them. The first thing she did was examine Laura's outfit and then she made a disgusted face. It was safe to say that she did not like Laura. She kissed his son but not her. In fact, she didn't even speak a word to Laura. There goes her chance of causing a good impression with his family.

James didn't let go of her hand yet, and she appreciated that. They all made way into his father, who was sitting in a modern wheelchair. He was sick, but his condition must have gotten worse because he was still walking at last year's event. He also took a very good look at Laura, but he expressed his disdain.

"Who the hell is that?", he asked James.

Laura wanted to speak for herself, but she let James take the lead.

"This my girlfriend, Laura.", he said.

Girlfriend? They barely even know each other. All the previous concerns that she had towards him came back and she felt used again. Maybe she was just a mere puppet for this stupid party. She let go of his hand and excused herself out. James followed her.

"Hey! Where are you going?", he shouted.

She went outside, away from all the fuss on the entrance and James soon catches up with her.

"Are you okay?", he asked her.

"I am your girlfriend?", Laura asked upset.

James relaxed his muscles and took a deep breath.

"Listen, my father is a very complicated person. I had to say that. I'm sorry."

"Do I even mean anything to you? Or am I just a prop for this stupid party?"

"No, it's not that.", James denied.

"Oh no?", she shouted, without being able to hold her tears anymore. "I know this is crazy, but you actually had me feeling something for you!", she confessed.

James seemed surprised and he got closer to Laura, holding her in his arms again. She was incredibly mad at him, but somehow his hug was so soothing that she could not refuse it. She felt safer in his arms, she did not feel alone anymore.

"I know this is all too much...", he started, whispering. "And I know that this is also crazy, but I feel something for you too. In just a day, I feel like I got to know the real you. You're different than everyone else that I've ever been with.".

His words resonated with Laura more than she wanted. Was he speaking the truth? She couldn't look at him now, because she had her face stuffed in his shoulder, but she holds him tighter. She did not want all of that to be a lie, and she didn't want to lose him.

"Let's get out of here.", he suggested.

She pulled herself together, wiped her tears and nodded positively. Getting away from all that stupid party was something that she would enjoy. James took her trough an alternative path to the garage, away from any cameras.

Since neither of them knew where they should go next, Laura suggested that they could go to her place, to which he agreed. Her house was simple but comfortable. However, it would be quite strange for them since her mother is living there. Suddenly, her idea didn't seem to be that good anymore.

"Actually, I totally forgot that my mom is staying with me know.", she said.

"It's okay. I actually want to show you something near your place.", he promised.

Laura was quite intrigued. Does this have anything to do with his presence at her neighborhood the other night? Whatever it was, Laura was glad that he would tell her about it. There was still a part of her that was skeptical about all of this. Is love at first sight even real? What if this feeling she has for him is not even love? Whatever it was, she was enjoying it. She felt like she knew him for a long time and that she could trust him.

James grabbed her hand while he was driving, and, once again, intertwined his finger with hers.

"I have a question to ask you.", he announced.

"Go ahead.", she said.

"What if you were my girlfriend... Would that be so bad?"

Laura's heart was racing so much that she was sure that he could feel it from her hand. Laura dating James Harris? It is a bit unreal. But isn't that what they are doing right now? They are holding hands, nonetheless. But dating is a strong word for Laura.

"Don't be ridiculous. He doesn't know each other that well…", she said honestly.

James laughed.

"You know what's so different about you?", he asked. "Every other girl that I've met wants to go to bed with me in the first few minutes and marry the next day. And you think it's too soon to call you my girlfriend."

"Because it is too soon. I don't care about your status or wealth. I am a bit uncomfortable with it, to be honest. What do you even see in me that would make you want to be my boyfriend?"

"You're so much more attractive than you think. Especially as a person. You have such a unique and raw personality. You don't pretend to be someone else when you're with me. That makes what we have real. That made me fall in love with you increasingly during this night. You're special to me, and I don't want to lose you."

His words were so sounding so truthful that she believed him. And now she was positive that he felt something for her too.

Chapter Six

They showed up at Laura's area and James halted at one of the houses directly before her.

"I was hesitant to let you know this since you may imagine that I was a stalker, however I purchased this property.", James said, pointing at the house before them. "I had no clue about that you lived simply nearby. No doubt!".

Laura chuckled.

"I trust you... ", she said. "That house has been on the lookout for a couple of months at this point. Be that as it may, for what reason did you need to purchase a house here?"

James breathed out and turned away.

"Since I need to move away from my family... I need to escape the organization. I need out of everything and carry on with my life how I need it.".

She could perceive that James was extremely disturbed with regards to it and that it was difficult for him to examine this matter. She likewise comprehended his reasons and she presumed how confounded his life was. She was additionally very glad that he would be residing simply nearby to her home. It would surely improve things among them and permitted them to get to know one another for the following not many days.

"That is the reason you were unable to tell anybody. I don't need them to know where I reside.", he clarified.

"Will you be fleeing from them?"

"As it were, definitely. Yet, I will in any case visit them, I simply need to secure one more position and abandon all of that. They won't ever uphold me however, so they will most likely be the ones who'll need me to flee from them."

"Please accept my apologies... ", she said, holding his hand more tight.

"It's alright. I truly need to do this.", he said, placing on a constrained grin. "Will we head inside?", he asked her.

Laura gestured decidedly.

The house was costly, she realized that since she had seen the promotion on the web. Within, it was at that point enlivened with all that his cash could purchase. The furniture was exceptionally present day, rich however basic, it was a comfortable spot.

James was doing a visit through the house when abruptly his room's light detonated, removing the power from the entire house.

"Are you OK?", he asked her.

"Indeed.", she answered.

It was completely dark and neither of them realized the house alright to move around in it. Additionally, they had left their telephones on top of his lounge table, so they couldn't utilize them. James held her body in his arms and both of their breaths promptly strengthened. Without acknowledging, Laura had her face contacting his and she out of nowhere felt his lips tasting hers.

It felt astounding. They were kissing on one another lips and, surprisingly fast, their tongues were at that point moving within their mouths. She was taking hold of James' body like paste and she was letting free all the craving that she was hanging on for a large portion of her life. Laura got his head with her hands and escalated their kiss.

Then, at that point, she took her hands to his midriff, feeling his muscular strength on the way down. He had his suit on, so she unfastened his jacket and took it off. James pushed her against the divider and she groaned a bit. She had never groaned; all things considered, she never at any point had intercourse. She utilized a couple of sex toys to engage herself, nonetheless, so it wouldn't be just terrible.

James started to take off her shirt, uncovering that she just had her bra under. She then, at that point, continued to take off his shirt, unfastening everything. It was such a large number of buttons! The two of them giggled and afterward he held her head with his hand, kissing her again.

She had as of now felt his faux pas as they scoured their horny bodies against one another, so she unfastened his jeans and took them off. She was unable to see everything except she could feel, with the center of her hand, the state of his hard penis and she could see that it was a major chicken.

Laura got on her knees and put her face near that gem, kissing it and contacting it with her hands. James was beginning to groan a bit and he put his hands on her head, stroking her hair. She removed his briefs, making his hard dick skip and hit his gut.

Shockingly, his dick smelled astonishing. He probably utilized a decent shower gel. She kissed it with her lips, feeling its delicate skin and afterward she opened her mouth to get it. She could take it. James was presently groaning noisily and his hand developments on her hair showed that he was adoring it.

The way that she was the justification for the joy that he was believing, was enough for her. She continued to speed up and she even got her hand out to help as she's found in pornography motion pictures.

"Hang on. I'm close.", James said.

Yet again he pulled her up and kissed her lips. The flavor of his penis was presently blended in with the two of them. James unfastened her bra and eliminate it from her body. Her bosoms were not little, but rather they weren't that huge by the same token. He put every one of his hands on every one of her boobs, holding them and pressing them delicately. Then, at that point, he started to kiss her neck, moving along to her stomach. Laura actually had her jeans on, so James additionally eliminated them.

Like how she had treated him, he started to kiss her clothing and feeling her pussy. She never had somebody going down on her and his lips against her labia felt astounding. He pulled her underwear from her body and kissed her vagina delicately. Then, at that point, he licked it. That was an inclination that she never felt. His wet tongue was making her vibrate. James licked it somewhat more and afterward, with the assistance of his fingers, set it within her. His tongue was vanishing within her vagina and she started to groan noisily.

She felt near coming as well, so she halted him. The two of them clasped hands and began to contact everything around them, to track down the bed. When she had the option to feel the sleeping cushion, she was maneuvered onto it, with her back laying on its delicate sheets and with James on top of her.

They kissed and she started to feel his dick scouring against her vagina. She could feel his warm breath all over and she was prepared for him to put it within her. She grasped her hand to his rooster and pushed it to her pussy, making it go in.

Laura shouted.

"Is everything OK?", James asked, exhausted.

"Definitely.", she told him.

Laura didn't have the foggiest idea why she shouted, perhaps in light of the fact that she had never felt anything like that.

His lips stuck onto hers and James began to speed up. Her body was in paradise! She was attempting to groan noisily, yet his mouth was holding her tongue hostage. She could hear James groaning and breathing intensely as well. They were both close.

"I'm going to cum.", James said.

"Try not to stop.", asked Laura, near peak as well.

The two of them shouted this time, as they all the while came. She could feel his cum pouring within her and his dick throbbing as he shouted. Their breaths were extremely discernible that they sort of seemed as though canines.

James removed his dick from her and lay in bed adjacent to her. They were both gazing into outright murkiness, yet they were both the most joyful individuals on the planet. Laura wasn't certain of things to come had coming up for her, however she realized that she needed to be close by. Furthermore realize she realizes that he needs exactly the same thing as well. The beyond couple of days, her life was over and above anyone's expectations previously and today, was the most joyful day of her life.

THE END

www.ingramcontent.com/pod-product-compliance
Lightning Source LLC
Chambersburg PA
CBHW071455150726
48000CB00006B/2562